Sue Hampton used to be a teacher and is grateful to all the children who inspired her and made her laugh. Now she enjoys meeting young people in schools and getting fan mail.

Sue's favourite things are flowers, gardens, woodland and Florence. Among her literary heroes are Shakespeare, George Eliot, Ted Hughes, Michael Morpurgo and Siobhan Dowd.

Illustrations by Jean M. A. Robinson

By the same author

'Spirit and Fire'
(Nightingale Books) 2007
ISBN 978 1 903491 58 4

'Voice of the Aspen'
(Nightingale Books) 2007
ISBN 978 1 903491 60 7

'Shutdown'
(Nightingale Books) 2008
ISBN 978 1 903491 59 1

'Just For One Day'
(Pegasus) 2008
ISBN 978 1903490 37 2

The Lincoln Imp

Sue Hampton

The Lincoln Imp

Pegasus

PEGASUS PAPERBACK

© Copyright 2009
Sue Hampton

The right of Sue Hampton to be identified as author of
this work has been asserted by her in accordance with the
Copyright, Designs and Patents Act 1988

A CIP catalogue record for this title is
available from the British Library

ISBN-978 1 903490 38 9

Pegasus is an imprint of
Pegasus Elliot MacKenzie Publishers Ltd.
www.pegasuspublishers.com

First Published in 2009

Pegasus
Sheraton House Castle Park
Cambridge CB3 0AX England

Printed & Bound in Great Britain

To Leslie x

Chapter One

JAKE HAD GROWN! The aunties, great aunties and fake aunties who arrived for the party all said so, one after the other or at the same time. But then, they hadn't seen him for years so it couldn't be much of a surprise. In any case, they soon got over their shock. They all hurried past him to meet the star of the show... the reason for the celebration... the smallest, loudest person in the room. Sunny.

Jake thought Sunny was growing by the second. It must be all that milk he kept sucking, his fingers spread out and his mouth locked on tightly. Jake reckoned that if you could look through a window in his brother's tummy you would see a great lake of milk, enough to float a rubber duck.

Jake's dad had said that if he kept growing at this rate Sunny might catch Jake up one day. But Jake wasn't going to let himself be caught. For the moment his brother was just a baby and babies couldn't catch anything except germs. If you threw a ball at Sunny, it would just smack him on the nose and make him howl.

His mum said Sunny couldn't see anything that wasn't right there in front of his face. That meant his world was all light and darkness, soft toys and fingers. It was also full of his own smells. And, drowning out everything else, his own NOISE.

Dad said babies don't *think* as much as *need*. And what they need they want immediately, straight away, at once and NOW! Otherwise they make the loudest fuss and they don't stop until they get it. If Jake tried that, he'd get sent to his room and no one would dream of giving in. It would be BAD BEHAVIOUR. Jake hadn't understood before, but he knew now: babies were allowed to break all the rules.

In any case Jake decided he must be growing at least as fast as Sunny. Not so long ago he had needed the plastic step to reach the kitchen sink. Now he could reach to turn the tap and fill a beaker. Jake was hot but the air was less sticky in the kitchen. The lounge was full of people and Sunny's wasn't the only face that was red.

Jake was glad to be on his own for a moment. The water tasted cool and the noise from the lounge sounded different now that he wasn't in the middle of it. Even Sunny's crying was much less sharp. It didn't burst inside Jake's head any more.

Jake couldn't think why his mum and dad had chosen to call the new baby Sunny when he never stopped wailing.

"More like Rainy!" he'd said. "More like Thunder!"

They'd laughed, but Sunny's crying wasn't really funny. Especially in the night when it woke everybody up.

Jake drank the water, looking out of the window at the back garden. It was cold out there, but he'd rather be outside with frozen ears than have to go back to the lounge. It smelt of wine and icing sugar and it was bulging like a Christmas stocking.

Jake loved his garden. It wasn't big or smart. Mum said it reminded her of a book Jake liked and called it *Where the Wild Things Grow*. It wasn't a designer garden. Nobody planned it. Trees were free to be trees. Jake's dad didn't believe in giving weeds a hard time and they were so grateful they danced all over the place. Mum said it was time he sorted them out (the way Daleks sorted enemies out) but Dad said he'd got other priorities. That meant Sunny. Sunny was number one PRIORITY. Jake supposed *he* was probably number two but it didn't feel the same. It was like a team trying to enjoy being top of the Championship when they used to be in the Premier League.

At the moment, Jake's back garden was buried. He couldn't only *see* autumn. He could hear it. The garden was shuffly and snuffly with leaves scattered by wind. They were crisp and curly and cracked like torn tissue paper but the colours were still as hot as a bonfire.

It was a fluttery garden and the wind was as wild as a tiger in a cage and trying to roar. The swings swayed as if ghost children sat on them.

The lid on the sandpit was rattling.

The flappy shirts on the washing line looked as if they might tug away from the pegs and lift off like swans. Jake imagined climbing inside those long, man-sized sleeves and flying away.

The wildness of the wind made Jake want to fight it. He put on his wellies and turned the key in the back door. No one heard. There was too much noise at the party.

Jake was kicking leaves. His football might be buried somewhere.

No one could beat the goalie with a shot of leaves. Beckham wouldn't be able to make them bend or curve over the keeper's head. They were like Sunny. They didn't do much. Jake wondered whether he would be the first boy to make a leafman because he couldn't wait for snow. He started to shape the base but some of the leaves were so floaty they just flew away again. Jake was chasing the annoying ones that wouldn't sit still when he heard a small thud behind him.

He thought it must be a conker so he crouched down to look for it. But he didn't find any conkers, acorns or dare-devil squirrels. Something had made the thud. But it wasn't the kind of something people expected to land in their back gardens. Jake stared. He closed his eyes for just a second before he opened them again. But it still looked just as real.

There, with two feet buried in leaves, stood a tiny, ugly kind of boy. But it wasn't like a human boy. For one thing it had no clothes. Its legs were fat as melted candles and its tummy looked full as a pillow. It was the colour of old stone that had been washed by rain.

Looking up slowly, Jake saw hands like fleshy claws that made him think of lizards. The creature was about as tall as a ruler and its head was no bigger than an apple, but not as smooth. It had all the wrinkles and creases of a little old man.

Jake knew what it was. He had seen that face high on the wall in the big old cathedral. He had seen it at the football ground, on badges and in shops. Everyone in Lincoln knew about the imp. But Jake had never expected it to jump down and visit him, or grin at him as if he was the funniest thing it had ever seen. Maybe those folds in his skin were cracks. Maybe when he leapt down to the cathedral floor he nearly broke. Or maybe since he'd landed he had changed, like caterpillars change to butterflies. This imp didn't look like he might smash to bits. He looked full of spring and bounce and rubbery stretch.

Jake didn't know which of them had stared the longest. He wondered whether the imp could see much more than Sunny. His narrowed eyes were low down, level with Jake's knees. But they were laughing at something.

Still smiling in a crooked sort of way, the imp began to run around grabbing leaves. He moved as fast as the wind itself. He scampered back towards Jake, spilling leafy clawfuls. Jake heard a laugh like a hiss with a gurgle in it.

Reaching up on tiptoe to the tops of Jake's wellies, the imp started to push the leaves down his boots! They didn't feel like the crisp, papery ones that wanted to be lighter than air.  They felt like the muddiest, soggiest, slimiest leaves in the garden and they made his socks squelch!

As the imp filled the space in the wellies his laugh grew louder. It sounded like a toad at the bottom of a bucket. Jake wobbled around trying to dodge away. Then he tipped like a seesaw with a Sumo wrestler sitting at one end. He sat on his bottom with a thump.

"It's not funny," said Jake, trying to pull off his boots.

When he tugged they felt as if they were stuck on with glue.

The imp thought it was very funny. His eyes were like shiny slits above his puffy cheeks.

Suddenly he was heading for the slide. He started to climb the ladder as if he had been practising for weeks. It was like Ronak and Owen climbing the ropes in gym and Mr Kite calling them spider monkeys. Jake didn't try to race him. He just sat there watching the imp slither down the slide with his arms spread wide like wings. His laugh grew throatier by the second.

As he slid off the bottom he floated above ground, sitting on the air with his fat legs crossed. It looked as if a tiny magic carpet held him up above the dirt and the puddles, until it tipped him softly onto grass. Jake remembered that in all the imp stories he arrived on the wind.

Jake hadn't been down the slide lately. Slime spread along it like old butter. Worse, there was a dip in the grass at the end, where Jake's feet had dug the earth away. It wasn't his fault that rain had filled it up with dark brown water. Dad had shouted last time Jake had landed in it. He'd said Mum had enough washing to do with Sunny's mess.

Jake followed the imp down the slide, planning to impress him with a leap over the mud at the end. It didn't work out that way. He landed in the puddle with soggy jeans to prove it. He might as well be wearing a wet nappy. But at least he didn't stink and he certainly wasn't going to cry.

As he looked around he expected to hear the imp laughing, but all he heard in the quietness was the grown-ups inside. The air felt still and there was no sign of the imp.

Jake lifted up leaves in case he was hiding underneath them. He looked behind the trees, but there was no impish face grinning anywhere. The wind blew up in a sudden rush. Jake felt cross. If Julia could see him she would tell him not to sulk. But the imp hadn't said goodbye. All he'd left behind was the wind whirling madly and the damp leaves still wedged in Jake's boots.

Then his dad was at the kitchen door, looking worried. Or possibly a little bit grumpy.

"What are you doing flinging yourself around the garden?" he called.

"Nothing," said Jake.

"You're filthy!" said his dad. "Come on in and be friendly."

"When are they going?" asked Jake. "I want to watch telly."

"Not yet," said his dad, closing the door behind Jake. "Don't start again."

"I'm not," said Jake.

He knew what he wasn't supposed to start. Dad had already told him twice before any of the guests arrived. He meant being moody. He meant being difficult. Jake had already said he wasn't being anything, but Dad didn't agree.

As Jake pulled off his boots he stared. They were empty. Not a leaf in sight. He looked at his socks and they weren't just mudless. They were spotless.

Jake stared out through the glass door into the garden at the wind tugging at the grass and shaking the flowers. On the other side of the glass he caught a glimpse of a small, grinning face near his dad's slippers. His impish nose was pressed flat and wide and his eyes were shiny as Christmas baubles. The imp was laughing. Jake could see his tummy shake as he giggled.

Then he tilted his neck to look up at Jake's dad, waved his claw-like fingers on the top of his head and stuck out a very long wobbly tongue. It was nearly as long and red as Jake's slide. Jake didn't know how he found room for a tongue like that in his apple-sized head.

Jake's mouth opened wide to let out a big laugh.

"Look, Dad!" he cried, pointing down at the little imp jumping up and down on the other side of the door.

He could hear the bouncy, breathless laugh through the glass.

"What?"

"There!"

"What?" said Dad again. "A woodlouse? WOW! Call the papers! Put it on the Ten O' Clock News!"

Jake looked. There *was* a woodlouse. It was crawling on the imp's bare foot but he didn't seem to mind. He was stroking it gently with a fat thumb. But Jake realised that his dad couldn't see the thumb, or the wrinkly feet, or the wide impish grin. In fact his dad couldn't see the imp at all.

But Jake could see. He wished he couldn't. The imp squeezed the woodlouse between his claw-like fingers. He opened his mouth and placed it inside as if it was a chocolate. Then he swallowed hard, but not all in one go. It looked as if the woodlouse got stuck somewhere. Jake thought all those wriggly legs must tickle. Perhaps they did, because the imp rubbed his tummy and laughed.

"Yuk!" said Jake, and shut his eyes in disgust.

When he opened them, the woodlouse wasn't the only thing that had disappeared. The imp had gone. So had one of his dad's big muddy gardening shoes, the ones he kept outside because they were so thick with mud that Mum wouldn't allow them indoors. Jake looked around the garden until he spotted it. It seemed to be sinking in the big puddle at the bottom of the slide. In fact it was filling up with dirty water like a ship about to sink.

"Hey!" cried his dad suddenly, charging out in his slippers to fetch it.

As Jake watched him reach for it, the shoe jumped out of the puddle and landed on the ground, just too far away for Dad to grab. Maybe the wind was stronger than Dad had thought.

Then the shoe sat very still, like a good boy in assembly, and let Dad pick it up. He tipped brown water out of it and shouted, "Oy!" on the doorstep.

There was a slug in the shoe, a big, fat, red-brown one. It was the biggest slug Jake had ever seen. It was so big he thought it might have fangs and drink blood. As his dad showed him, Jake bravely picked it out of the shoe and took it outside.

"This," he whispered into the wind, "is not for pudding."

His dad was putting the shoe on the radiator to dry.

Jake thought there would soon be quite a smell in the kitchen.

"What did you say, Jakey?"

"I said," said Jake, "this is some wind."

A loud howl travelled from the living room and got inside Jake's head.

"Talking of wind," said his dad, "I think Sunny's got some in his tummy."

Jake didn't feel too sorry for his baby brother. Whatever wind got up to in his tummy, it had to taste a lot better than woodlice. Or giant blood-sucking slugs.

He followed his dad back to the party.

Chapter Two

In the lounge Jake's sister Julia was trying to make Sunny stop crying and laugh instead. Julia spent a lot of time looking at Sunny as if he was an amazing new invention or a joke that never stopped being funny. She was always saying things like, "Look at his little fingers!" or "Look at his cute little toes!"

Today Julia was focusing on his nose.

"It's so small!" she was telling Great Auntie Kay. "It's like a little raspberry!"

Jake hoped the imp wouldn't agree, or he might want to eat that little raspberry nose.

Julia was wobbling around in silly heels and a strappy dress. She was looking at herself in every reflection she could find. Jake thought if she went outside in that cold wind she'd either freeze solid, or be blown around like a Tesco bag in a car park. It seemed to Jake that Julia wanted to be fourteen, but in fact she was nine.

"Saw you in the garden," she said. "Very weird!"

Jake just smiled. He was thinking of the imp and how Julia would scream at the sight of his ugly face.

"Sunny wants you to hold him," she said.

She started to pass the squirmy baby over to Jake while the aunties, great aunties and fake aunties all smiled and cooed at those little wriggly legs.

Jake had held Sunny on his lap once, at the hospital. He was in a small white blanket and all he did was sleep. He kept Jake warm as he slept, like his Scottish gran's fat old cat.

Now, when Jake put him on his shoulder, he smelt something bad. He held his brother as far away as possible from his best England shirt. Sunny's legs dangled in his new all-in-one stretch suit. Inside the padded feet he was trying to kick.

"Euoo!" cried Julia. "He's leaked on you! Right on the three lions!"

"WHAT?!"

Sunny was wriggling now, like an upside-down woodlouse with not so many legs. He was yelling and his yell was growing louder by the second. A football crowd could not have made more noise if England had just won the World Cup on penalties.

Jake saw that the badge on his shirt had no stains or trickles. There wasn't even any dribble where Sunny's mouth had rested on his shoulder. He glared at Julia, who was mouthing, "Gotcha!"

All over the room everyone had stopped talking and eating to look at the world's loudest baby. Jake's mum was hurrying to take Sunny, and looking at Jake with her eyebrows scrunched. Her eyes underneath felt a bit like lasers targeting him, as if to say *What have you done?*

"Not my fault," he said, looking hard at Julia.

Was Jake imagining it or had the smiles gone from everyone's faces? He felt like escaping to his room, but he knew no one would let him. They would say he was *starting* again. It wasn't fair. The way Mum and Dad were looking at him made Jake feel like that slug in Dad's shoe.

Julia went over to the table to fetch more food.

For someone who told Jake he should eat more healthily, Julia was putting away a lot of cake and crisps.

Just for a moment he thought he saw a small, ugly creature the size of a ruler running between Julia's legs, climbing the table leg and pulling at the table cloth. He blinked and the imp had gone. But Julia was wiping blackcurrant juice from her high-heeled shoes and staring at a plate of cup cakes that had landed on the floor. One cake was on the carpet with quite a wide bite missing from its pink crunchy top.

"Julia!" said Mum, more sharply than usual.

Julia said she hadn't done anything, but she cleared up the mess. She was looking rather sulky and Jake felt a bit sorry for her. He thought he knew whose sharp little teeth had made the marks in that pink icing. He put the rest of the cake in his mouth.

"I don't know what happened," said Julia, who didn't like being in trouble. "I'm never clumsy."

Somehow Jake heard the doorbell in spite of Sunny's screaming. He said he would get it because he hoped it was a special missing person. Yes! There was his grandfather, his thin grey hair messed and wild. His eyes looked watery. Maybe the cold wind had got into them, or maybe it was because he'd been in the graveyard over the road, talking to Jake's grandma.

"Sorry I'm late," said Grandad, sounding rather sniffily. He wiped his nose with a big old hanky. "There was such a lot to say," he explained. "Have I been missed?"

Jake just smiled and hugged him. Now that Grandad was here he realised he had missed him a lot.

"Grandma sends her love," said Grandad.

"I wanted to come with you," said Jake.

His mum and dad didn't think it was a good idea to talk to Grandma in her grave. Mum had let him go with her before Sunny was born. She had given Jake the flowers to put on the grave. Then she had stood there, silent and still, her hand on the bump that had been Sunny. There had been no wind that day but her eyes had been cloudy. Jake had tried not to cry because he thought he would make it worse for Mum, but his throat had been blocked and solid.

Grandad said he was going to visit Grandma every day. Maybe sometime he would take Jake too.

"But today's a special day. They wanted you here at the party," said Grandad.

Jake didn't know why. The party was for Sunny, even though he didn't seem to be enjoying it much.

"I'll just be sociable for a bit," said Grandad, "and then do you want to play Champions League?"

So they did, after Grandad had said hullo to everyone and loaded up a plate. Jake won. He always did, but Grandad was improving. Jake told him he just needed more practice.

"Grandma used to say that about me and the washing up," said Grandad. "And the ironing too. I'd get better with more practice. But I let her do it. I've been saying sorry."

"She forgives you," said Jake, because his grandma was great at forgiving.

"She'd say we should go back to the party. We mustn't be party poopers."

Jake told Grandad about the nappy and said Sunny was the pooper.

"So were you!" laughed Grandad. "So was your mum! Your grandma used to soak nappies in a bucket and scrub the stains. I remember a washing line full of them, blowing in the wind."

Jake nearly asked him as they went downstairs about windy days and whether he and Grandma had ever had any small, ugly visitors. In his head it sounded silly now.

The rest of the party was much more fun with Grandad there. His other grandparents had been there for hours, but they were stony. They sat like statues in the White Witch's castle, only moving to place sausage rolls in their mouths. Grandad wasn't like that. He behaved as if Aslan had just set him free and he was so glad he might cry. At one point he did a twirl on his toes that made Jake laugh out loud. He called it a pirouette.

"You were always dancing," Grandad reminded Jake's mum.

"Sunny might be a ballet dancer," she said. "Look at him go!"

Sunny's legs were all over the place as she held him out to be admired again. Jake reached for another cup cake, a white one that made him think of snow before anyone trod in it. He was feeling hungrier now.

"He might be a footballer. Our Sunny might play for Lincoln City," said Dad.

"If you're going to make any jokes about him being an imp," said Mum, "remember that everyone says he looks like you!"

"Jake's a cracking player, aren't you?" said Grandad. "A real hotshot!"

"Not really," said Jake, but he was glad Grandad remembered.

As Jake picked up the snow-topped cake, some kind of small wind whirled and spun above the table. When it slowed to a stop he saw it wasn't a wind at all. It was the imp. He was on his toes, doing a pirouette in the air.

Everything underneath him wobbled, leaned, slid or rattled. People stared. Other people rushed to catch things before they fell. The green jelly, which was dancing like a space monster, broke up with a squelch.

But Jake could tell that no one saw the imp. In the middle of the chaos he was laughing like a scouring pad scrubbing a pan.

Jake reached for another cup cake. It was then that he saw Grandad smiling at the space in the middle of the table where the imp had been. Perhaps he imagined it. Perhaps he imagined a lot of things.

"I think I brought the wind in with me," joked Grandad.

Later, when Sunny was sleeping, Grandad asked Jake to play the piano. He played his best Grade One piece, which he knew really well, but this time he hit some wrong notes. There were so many eyes on him that he felt warm and wobbly inside. But everyone clapped and Grandad said, "Marvellous!" as if he meant it.

Sunny didn't agree. Sunny started wailing. Jake was going to put the lid down when he heard a deep, sad sound at the left end of the keyboard. The imp had balanced on tiptoe on a very low black note. It seemed to echo all around the room. Then he leapt around the keyboard, playing four notes at once, two with his claw-like hands and two with his feet. He was looking at Jake and wiggling his bottom in the air. Jake tried not to laugh. In fact he tried not to fall off the piano stool!

It was wild and stormy music, or would have been, if it had been music at all. Great Auntie Kay pulled a face. Jake realised all everyone could see was his back. They thought *he* was playing!

"That's enough now, dear," said Auntie Kay.

Jake didn't like her all that much because she tried to make Grandad do things he didn't want to do, like move to a smaller place now that he was on his own.

"More than enough, Jake. Come away," said Dad.

"I thought it was rather fun," said Grandad. "So did Sunny. Look!"

It was true. Sunny's mouth had closed. He looked as if he was concentrating hard on something.

Then the imp jumped up to the top of the piano as if a gust of wind carried him. From there he leapt down like a parachute jumper (without a parachute). He was lying on the air on his tummy with his arms out wide, and the air held him up so that his fall was slow and floaty, like a leaf. As he fell, so did Auntie Kay's strawberry pink hat. She squealed and tried to catch it

but it dodged her and landed softly on the floor. There it was, like a safety net, for the imp to land in. Bang on target! Jake wanted to cheer.

But before he could do anything, the hat was on the move again. With its impish passenger, it glided around, hovering just above the carpet. He stirred the air with a teaspoon, as if it was a paddle and the hat was a canoe. He was having so much fun that his eyes shone. Every time Auntie Kay tried to lean down low enough to grab the hat the imp turned his boat around sharply and she missed.

Grandad was the one who simply reached out and picked the hat up. He gave it to Great Auntie Kay, who was his big sister. As he touched it the imp sprang out of it and disappeared. Grandad brushed the hat down and Auntie Kay smiled and put it on.

Julia glared at Jake as if somehow everything was his fault. But Sunny really had stopped crying, and that made everyone relax.

Jake thought the imp had gone, until out of the corner of his eye he saw something move on the table. A creamy, multi-coloured and very sticky creature clambered out of the trifle with a slice of banana stuck to his head. Using a long tongue that curled down, out and around, the imp licked himself all over. Then he licked his lips with a smacky noise. As he crept on tiptoe across the carpet he left a trail of sticky puddles behind.

The door blew open and the imp blew out of it, waving not once but twice. When Jake turned round, Grandad was staring at the door with a tear in his eye.

"I miss her," he said, and when he held out his hand, Jake squeezed it.

Grandad fetched a cloth to mop up the spills on the carpet. Sunny had fallen asleep very suddenly and very peacefully so Mum carried him up to his cot. Grandad organised some games and Jake cheered up. Julia stopped glaring at him and Mum and Dad seemed much happier. But of course it couldn't last.

It wasn't long before a small noise from upstairs swelled into a very loud cry indeed. Sunny returned, his face hot and his mouth twitchy and stretchy, ready to open wide. The aunties cleared up, chatting as loudly as they could in the kitchen. Then the party broke up. But Grandad stayed after everyone else had gone. While Dad took Sunny out in the pram and Mum had a lie down on the bed, Grandad told Jake a bedtime story.

"Once there was an imp..." he said, "who pretended to be an ordinary boy. He fooled just about everybody, but his grandfather knew. His grandfather knew about imps."

Jake grinned because he'd heard this story and the boy's name began with J.

"But there really is an imp," he said, listening to the

quietness and hoping Sunny wasn't about to come back and burst it open.

"I know," said Grandad, and winked.

Jake couldn't wink back. Winking was like tying shoe laces. His eyes, like his fingers, tried hard but made him feel silly.

Grandad started to tell the story of when Jake was born, but by the time he got to the christening party, Jake was asleep.

Chapter Three

Jake had known the story of the imp for a while. Everyone in Lincoln knew because people came from all over the world to find the carving in the cathedral. Jake's class had been there on a school trip when he was in Reception. It was an enormous place, bigger and higher than a castle. The old stone walls and pillars were carved with all sorts of shapes and patterns. The imp wasn't the only ugly face among the saints and the angels playing music. But he was certainly the most famous.

All around the imp there were leafy shapes. Jake thought they looked like Christmas sprouts, and the imp himself was so small and so high up that they almost hid him. Lots of children in the class couldn't find him at all even when the man in charge pointed. So the man let Ronak put twenty p in a slot. At once the imp lit up and everyone made noises like "Ah!" and "Oh!" and "Cool!"

Some of the girls thought he was cute but Samira cried because she said he had a nasty little face. Jake wasn't sure then. Maybe the imp looked mean. Or perhaps he only looked like what his grandma used to call *a bit of a scamp*. But Jake agreed with the man that he was fun.

"He's an odd surprise, isn't he," the man asked Jake and Ben, "in such an old, serious, grown-up place?"

"Yes," said Jake, but it came out like a whisper.

There were lots of stories but they were all about the imp being naughty. He was supposed to have been caught by an angel when he was causing trouble in the cathedral. He jumped up on top of a pillar and threw rocks at the poor angel, who wasn't very pleased and turned him to stone.

Throwing rocks at an angel was obviously a bad thing to do. Jake couldn't believe his imp would do anything so horrible.

"But you can't hurt angels, can you?" he had asked the man who showed them round. "They don't have skin and bones."

The man said he didn't know because he had never seen one. Lois said she had, in a film, and they had see-through wings of different colours.

Mrs Harper, the Reception teacher, said maybe Lois was mixing angels up with fairies but Lois said angels were bigger and didn't wear pink. Owen said angels were see-through all over and if you threw a rock at one it would go straight through and break a window.

"Now I think you're muddling up angels and ghosts," said the man.

This led to a few silly *ooo-ooo* noises and some people pulled faces that were meant to be scary.

Most of Jake's class seemed to agree that angels were like superheroes. You couldn't hurt one. So Jake said that in that case the imp hadn't done any harm.

He said it quietly, because when he started to talk and heard his voice in the big silence it always made him feel shy. Then his voice faded into a whisper, so no one took any notice. When his voice shrank Jake felt as if he was shrinking too. This time, though, Mrs Harper heard, and later on, on the bus back to school, she said that a thief was still a thief even if the purse he stole turned out to be empty.

Jake had a feeling she was talking about the imp. It was her way of saying he was guilty anyway, even if angels were made of air and as boneless as jelly. But Jake felt sorry for that stone imp high up on the wall looking down on the crowds below. He thought he must wish he could come down to play.

The man said one version of the story had two imps, both being naughty, but one got away. He didn't say anything about where it went.

Jake could not imagine the imp that visited him throwing a rock at anyone. Maybe a trifle or a pizza or one smelly (real life) sprout after another, but not rocks. Of course angels did not deserve to be pelted. Jake wasn't the kind of boy to throw anything, even a rubber across the table at school. He had thrown a teddy at Julia once, but she caught it, put a dress on it and wouldn't give it back for ages.

In the old days there was a punishment where people were supposed to throw things at the head of the person in trouble. It must have hurt because the person being punished had to stand leaning his head out of a hole in something called the stocks. The things people threw were disgusting and mouldy.

Nowadays there was a fun version at school fairs with a hole in a big board and wet sponges to throw. Mr Kite volunteered last time and everyone was jumping up and down, desperate to have a go. When his turn was over his hair was dripping, his shirt was soaked and he pretended to rub his eyes with his fists and cry like a baby. Mr Kite was a great teacher and actually he was having fun. But Jake thought some people really did deserve to be pelted with *something*.

He made a target list in his head.

Julia, but only sometimes. She could be kind when she remembered.

One of the lunchtime supervisors, because she screwed up her face as if she thought the children were as disgusting as the food.

His annoying cousin, Emily, even though she hadn't annoyed him for a while because she was on holiday in Austria.

But top of the list was Mrs Grey. She was mean and moody and grumpy and miserable. She lived next-door with a black cat that was even fiercer than she was. It was frizzy, as if its claws had been slotted into a socket on a wall and electricity had passed all the way from the tip of its tail to its wiry whiskers.

Mrs Grey called the cat Pet. Jake thought that even though she had an extra-large temper her vocabulary must be very small. Pet was a very feeble name. If he had a cat like that he would call it Hiss or Sizzle or Zap.

Pet the cat was always sleeping on Jake's family's flower bed. Unfortunately sleeping was not all it did. Jake's mum and dad were not too happy about having to bury the dollops the cat left behind. They had to get the trowel to bury them, but they didn't go next door to complain. It was Mrs Grey who did all the complaining.

She had a way of knocking that sounded like the police had come to arrest someone or the Big Bad Wolf was trying to batter the house into a pile of sticks. Mrs Grey was always knocking about something.

"I can't hear the television when there are children in the garden."

"That paddling pool just encourages noise! Splashing and squealing and laughter! It really is too much."

"Does the boy have to kick a ball against the wall like that? It gives me such a headache."

For someone who hated noise so much Mrs Grey spent a lot of time banging on Jake's front door.

Jake's mum said that Mrs Grey wasn't very old. She said she wished she would brighten herself up with some colourful clothes. Jake thought her eyes would look old and tired even if she wore a pink mini skirt, purple tights and silver shoes.

His dad said however old or young she was, she had obviously never been a child. She'd popped out of her mother's tummy wearing glasses and a frown, complaining that it was much too noisy in there.

After Sunny had arrived home from the hospital, and started crying half the night and most of the day, Jake's family had waited for the complaints to start. But no! The first time Mrs Grey met Sunny he was twisting up his face in the pram as if he was trying hard to fill his nappy.

"What a fine-looking fellow!" she cried. She actually smiled.

A few days later she had heard Sunny howling from inside while she swept up her leaves.

"What a powerful pair of lungs!" she called over the fence, as if she thought Jake's mum and dad should be very proud to be the parents of the world's loudest baby.

In fact when it came to the youngest member of the family, Mrs Grey was just as wide-mouthed and round-eyed as everybody else.

They had invited her to the party, so that she couldn't complain about the noise of people talking and laughing.

"I don't like parties," she said, her nose lifting from her down-turned mouth as if she'd just tasted toad soup.

Jake wondered whether she had, because she did look a bit like a witch. Maybe she kept a cauldron in her kitchen.

Mrs Grey was definitely mean.

The day after the party was as windy as ever but the sun was bright. On the other side of the fence Mrs Grey was hanging out washing. Jake was in the garden making a den. Some of Sunny's giant presents had been packed in enormous boxes and Dad had said Jake could have them. He was making lookout holes and a chute so that his Lego men could slide out in an emergency.

The card was thick and he was using the big scissors and all his strength. Maybe Mrs Grey didn't like the noise of the card tearing, or maybe it was Jake's humming that upset her. It was supposed to be the Thunderbirds tune and it made his head shake backwards and forwards as he hummed it.

"It goes right through me," she called. "Make your nasty noise inside!"

Jake pretended he hadn't heard. He stopped humming and opened his mouth wide: "NA NANA NA! NANA NA NA NA NANA NA NA NA!"

"No manners at all!" she grumbled to herself.

Later on, when the den was finished, Ben came round to play in it. Ben was mostly Jake's best friend. He was taller than Jake and his voice was deeper. He had a teenage brother and liked music Jake had never heard of. He couldn't believe Jake had never had a curry called a vindaloo.

"It blows your head off!" he said, as if that was a good thing.

"I like custard," said Jake.

Custard left his head alone and felt like a hot water bottle inside his tummy. Mum hadn't had time to make it since Sunny arrived.

Ben said Jake's den was "Awesome!" and thought Head Case would love it. Head Case was his nickname for his very active hamster, even though his parents called him Harry. Ben's hamster liked to fill his cheeks with food for later, so they were always the size of golf balls.

Ben brought the hamster outside but Head Case ignored the chute. He made straight for the lookout holes. But they weren't as round as he was. He wriggled and squidged, but he was stuck. He did look very funny, with his fat cheeks and his legs dangling. But it was an emergency.

Mrs Grey didn't understand.

"Can you cut down that awful noise?" she called. "Now!"

They pushed the hamster's bottom from behind. They tried to pull his front legs through on the other side. He was wedged tight. Ben got the scissors to try to make the hole bigger but Ben's face turned white in case Jake cut something he shouldn't. Jake put the scissors down.

Down on the breeze plopped the imp, hands on hips. He waved hullo to Jake and he waved to the hamster. Ben didn't see a thing, but the hamster must have seen. Head Case, who didn't seem too bothered about the emergency, waved a front leg back.

The imp had a creased-up think. Then, puffing up his cheeks, he pretended to pop them with two claw-like fingers. Head Case was not so daft. At once he did the same. He emptied his cheeks and slid smoothly down from the hole. Ben stroked him over and over again.

As for the imp, he unrolled his tongue, scooped up the splodge of hamster food from Head Case's cheeks and rubbed his tummy.

"Euooo! Gross!" cried Jake.

"What?" asked Ben.

"Nothing," said Jake.

Ben took Head Case indoors to his cage and when Jake looked round the imp had gone.

Maybe Mrs Grey would have stayed indoors if the Daleks had not tried to attack the den. Ben could do a really good Dalek impression. Jake's dad pretended to hide behind the sofa whenever he heard it. Jake wished Mrs Grey had done the same, and stayed there. For ever.

"This won't do, you know!" she called, the loudest voice of all.

Her voice sounded like a key scratching the paintwork on a car.

"I can't put up with all this noise! I'll complain to the council! I'll call the police!"

Her face over the top of the fence was much scarier than a Dalek. Ben said his tea must be ready. His big brother came to walk him home.

So Jake sat in his den with his arms folded and his fists closed as tightly as his mouth. The sun had gone away and the air felt colder. He hoped the imp might come back again, even if he was more trouble than a slightly mad hamster.

Maybe the imp read Jake's mind. As Jake stared at the walls of the den, he climbed through the jagged look-out hole one leg at a time. He didn't get stuck. Using his fists and his claw-like feet, he just burst through like a drill, scattering bits of cardboard into the den like coffee-coloured snow. He tumbled down onto the old cushion, making a noise like a gust of wind through a pipe.

He bounced and landed a few times, filling the air with dust. Then he put a claw-like finger to his wrinkly lips. His eyes flamed like firelight.

He had gone. All Jake felt was the wind, flowing like a wave across his garden and over the fence into the garden next-door. He pressed his face to a thin crack in the wood that he tried to use as a spy-hole. But all he could really see was whiteness, as the washing billowed and swung on Mrs Grey's line.

Suddenly his football lifted from the grass beside him and soared high over the fence. Jake took a moment to understand, but only a moment. It was a signal. It meant that somebody small and ugly wanted him to come.

Two minutes later he was standing on Mrs Grey's doormat. It didn't say KNOCK IF YOU DARE in red letters at his feet. Jake dared, and waited. She took her time. When she appeared she looked angry.

"Please, Mrs Grey, my football went over your fence."

The noise she made was her tongue beating against the inside of her teeth.

"Can I go round and get it, through the side gate," he asked, "to save you going out in the cold?"

This time the noise she made was more like a growl, as if something fierce and furry was stuck in her throat.

"Be quick," she said. "I'm busy."

Mrs Grey let her words out like dogs from a kennel, fast and sharp and yapping.

Jake went through the gate just as the wind turned the sheets into a Mexican wave. The imp balancing on the line didn't need to point. Jake saw. All over the whiteness a trail of colour was scattered. It was like spilt fire, red, gold and orange. Leaves were glued all over Mrs Grey's washing. It was so wild and beautiful Jake thought it should hang in an art gallery where everyone would admire the pattern and the colour. But it only hung on Mrs Grey's line. And so did the imp, who was swinging like a gymnast. He dropped down with a light bounce and a loud laugh.

The imp's claw-like hands were brown with slimy, rainy mud. It was the mud that held the pattern in place. He looked very proud, like an artist smiling on his work.

Jake grabbed the ball to his chest and scuttled back through the gate as if his favourite pizza was on the table. Back in his den he did not dare laugh. He hardly dared breathe. He just sat waiting for an earthquake ... for a thunderstorm ... for Mrs Grey to fire out words like bullets from a gun.

But all he heard, after the warning beat of feet on the stone path, was tears. It wasn't wailing or howling. It wasn't Sunny, not this time.

Mrs Grey was crying.

Chapter Four

Jake opened up his reading folder and took out his book, but inside his head he could still hear Mrs Grey crying. He couldn't concentrate on The Finger Eater even though it did look rather like the imp in a very bad mood. He asked his mum and dad what was the matter with Mrs Grey.

"How long have you got?" asked his dad. "It's quite a list. She's got a screw loose if you ask me."

Julia looked up from the story she was writing.

"No she hasn't," she said. "She likes me. She told me last week that I looked pretty."

"What do you think, Jakey?" grinned Dad. "Shall we put poor eyesight at the top of the list?"

"And a screw loose!" cried Jake, laughing.

"Hey!" protested Julia, and threw a cushion. It might have been meant for Dad or it might have been meant for Jake, but it missed. Julia was smiling. She didn't mind being teased. Dad said teasing was attention and that was what Julia liked best.

"I think Mrs Grey is all right," she said. "She's just unhappy."

"I think," said their mum, "that she's lost someone."

"Like Mr Grey?" Jake suggested.

"If there was a Mr Grey," said his dad, "she probably chopped him up and put him in the freezer." He grinned. "He probably snored too loudly ... laughed too loudly ... or breathed too loudly!"

Jake's mum told Jake that his dad was only joking.

"Someone said Mr Grey left ..." she began.

"I don't blame him!" interrupted Jake's dad, sitting upright because of the cricket on screen. "No!" he groaned as another England player was caught out.

"Shhh!" said Jake's mum, her eyes to the ceiling, because above them Sunny was asleep.

"Shall I hear you read?" Julia asked Jake.

"Would you, love?" said Mum. "That's really kind of her, isn't it, Jakey?"

Jake supposed so. Julia wanted to be a teacher. She became kind and patient and helpful when she listened to him read. She helped him work out words he didn't know.

He read four pages of The Finger Eater and she told him he'd done very well. Then she went back to her own story and made him promise to listen to it when she'd finished. Jake didn't mind. Her stories were full of surprises and jokes.

"What are you going to do today, Jakey?" asked his mum.

It was nearly the end of half term. Before Sunny, she didn't ask him what he was going to do. She made suggestions. It wasn't so easy now to go out for the day, to get a train to London or go to see a film.

"Grandad will have Emily today," she said. "You haven't seen her for a while."

Emily was Jake's cousin. Her dad, Uncle Mike, was Mum's brother. The family had missed Sunny's party because they were flying back from a skiing trip, but Jake hadn't missed Emily.

She was only four months older than him but her handwriting was perfect. She could spell words he hadn't even heard of and double numbers in her head. And double them again. More than anything Emily liked made up, acting games, and sometimes she didn't seem to know the difference between pretend and real.

"I'm a princess and you're a frog," she told him once.

"Do I change into a prince?" asked Jake, hoping he wouldn't have to marry her.

"No," she said, as if he was very silly, "you're just a frog. You get squashed under the wheels of my carriage."

Another time she had wanted to be a doctor and operate on Jake with a lot of colourful plastic tools. He didn't mind at first but when he tried to get off the operating table she held him down. She told him he would bleed to death because she hadn't sewn him up yet. Then she sewed with a long, slow, poking fingernail.

Emily was bossy. But when Grandad was there, she hogged his lap and put bows in his wispy hair. She called him the gentle giant and he seemed sad, but happy too. Jake thought the gentle giant had room on his lap for two, but Emily seemed to forget Jake was there. She only remembered when she needed a servant to fetch her things or a dog to pat.

Still, Jake always liked to see Grandad, and Ben was out for the day, so he said yes. He'd put up with Emily. She was all right when she was just a freckled girl in jeans and in the mood to climb a tree.

Dad drove him round to Grandad's house and offered to sweep up leaves, because the garden was buried under them, but Grandad said the three of them would build some pyramids later.

The house was tidy, just the way Grandma used to keep it, smelling of fresh air and flowers. When Grandad and Jake decided to bake a cake, all kinds of other flavours blended in the kitchen. Chocolate and vanilla sweetness warmed the air. They were spreading icing on the top and taking turns to lick the spoon when there was a ring on the doorbell.

While Grandad went to let Emily in, there was a sudden current of air from nowhere, followed by a splat. A smaller, uninvited visitor landed in the mixing bowl. The imp seemed very pleased to see Jake. He was throbbing with excitement and his tongue was hanging out. But then Jake saw that his eyes were glinting at the sight of all that sweetness waiting to be slurped and swallowed. It was the icing he was pleased to see.

Soon it coated his puffed cheeks and clung to his knobbly chin. It filled his pointy ears. It stuck between his claw-like toes and made it hard for them to grip the worktop. In fact he lost his balance, tumbled, slid and spun out of control. Jake put his hands out like buffers to stop a runaway train. Then he wrapped them around him, lifted him up and hoped he wouldn't nip.

Jake sat him in the washing up bowl. There the imp splashed bubbled water up at him, and laughed when Jake ducked and said "Oy!" He was trying to bath him the way his mum bathed Sunny, but the imp wouldn't keep still. He didn't make as much noise but he was ten times messier.

Emily came into the kitchen at the point of maximum mess. Icing smeared the surfaces. Water puddled the floor.  Jake's face and hair were wet and there were bubbles on his nose. One got stuck in a nostril and tickled till it burst and made him sneeze. The imp ducked out of the way under the water, and jumped up again like a whale surfacing. There was a giant splash.

Of course Emily didn't see the imp at all, not even when he stuck out his tongue at her as he jumped up and down in the bubbles.

"Grandad," she said, "Jake's flooding the kitchen."

Grandad just told the two of them to play in the other room while he cleared up. Jake couldn't be sure, but he thought he heard Grandad talking to someone in the kitchen. He hoped the imp was helping, riding the mop over the floor.

In the living room Emily picked up the framed photo of Grandma and started to cry quietly. Jake didn't know what to do or say.

"You're lucky," she told him. "I wish I had a baby to play with."

Jake told her you couldn't play with babies. They were useless. But Emily wasn't listening. She was searching in her big play bag. Then she announced her idea, a let's pretend idea. She wanted Jake to be her baby brother.

Her baby doll had mini nappies. They would have wrapped twice around the imp, but they wouldn't stretch round Jake's jeans however hard Emily pulled. Emily was very disappointed. Jake wasn't.

But the dummy that slotted into a hole in the doll's mouth fitted Jake perfectly. It sat between his lips in a way that made Emily smile and clap. When he took it out she put it back in again.

"We need a blanket to wrap you in," said Emily, and used the throw that hid the oldness of the sofa.

Jake said it was itchy.

"Don't be a baby!" said Emily, and laughed at her joke.

Jake didn't laugh, even before she put the dummy back in his mouth again. He felt like a sausage being coated in pastry. He felt like the bean sprouts in a spring roll, hot and damp and trapped.

"Pooh!" said Emily. "Your nappy needs changing, baby!"

Jake took his dummy out.

"No it doesn't! I'm not a baby. I don't want to play any more."

"Babies don't talk!" Emily objected. "Be a good icky baby and go to sleep."

Jake would not have minded going to sleep if he had thought that when he woke up Emily would be gone.

"Waaaa!" he cried instead. "Waaa waa waaa!"

But Emily wasn't cross. She loved it. She thought Jake was playing his part really well.

"Good acting!" she whispered, right in his ear.

Jake wiped the wetness out. His ear wasn't the only place that felt damp. He could feel the start of a tear inside his eye and he didn't want her to see it leak out.

Grandad didn't come. He was taking a phone call now. He was probably glad they were getting on so well and playing nicely.

But the imp knew better.

Emily never saw so much as a glimpse of him, but her mouth opened in shock as she felt the dummy land in her right ear. A second dummy flew out of her play bag and popped itself into the left. The two dummies stuck out of the side of her head like Frankenstein's monster's bolts. Emily's eyes could not have opened any wider if she had been watching a horror film.

A sudden wind caught the itchy throw, unwrapped Jake and rolled it around Emily. It rolled her so fast that she spun down onto the floor and rolled some more.

Everything happened so quickly that Jake just sat with an open mouth that didn't quite let go of the word, "No!"

The imp was pointing a fat finger at Emily and laughing. He was hopping from one foot to another and slapping his rubbery thighs. Jake didn't think he heard Emily whimpering as if she'd just been sick, or noticed how red and white her face looked.

With a chuckle in his little throat, the imp was gone.

Grandad came into the room in time to see Emily start to cry inside the rolled-up throw. She wasn't being a good actress. It was real. Her face was as red as a baby's but she wasn't scrunching it up and howling. She was sobbing softly.

Grandad freed and hugged her. Then he brushed her hair and blew her nose for her. Jake wanted them both to know it wasn't his fault. The imp was sticking up for him. Emily shouldn't be so bossy. She should treat him with respect. But he didn't want her to cry like that. It made him feel heavy in his chest.

He went into the kitchen and found a bite-sized hole in the cake. He cut a slice round it and ate it quickly but he didn't enjoy it. Then he cut two more slices.

When he gave the cake to Grandad and Emily, they both said thank you but neither of them smiled.

"It wasn't my fault," said Jake.

"Nobody in this room meant to upset anyone," said Grandad.

Jake knew what he meant. He was blaming the imp. But had the imp meant to upset Emily? He'd only copied her. He'd only defended Jake. It wasn't fair.

"Let's gather up those leaves," said Grandad, giving Emily a kiss on the cheek.

He reached his arms out to Jake, who held onto him tightly.

"Just the three of us," he added, in a slower, louder voice — almost as if he thought someone else might be listening.

Chapter Five

Half term was over.

"Thank goodness!" said Jake's dad, sweeping his forehead with the back of his hand. "Peace and quiet!"

Sunny howled at that, so nobody would forget that there was no getting rid of him.

Julia was happy to go back to school because she had new shoes, and a new fluffy pencil case with feet and goggle eyes. Besides, she was looking forward to seeing all her friends.

Jake would have liked school better if he felt bigger there. Once he was in the classroom he couldn't find a loud enough voice to help him be himself. His teacher, Mr Kite, was young and kind. He said his writing used to be hard to read too, when he was in Year Two.

Mr Kite was artistic and sporty. Jake wasn't the best footballer in the class but he could make clay do whatever he wanted it to. Mr Kite usually mounted his paintings and displayed them on the classroom wall. He said Jake had a "great feel for colour." So did Mr Kite because he wore ties that looked as if someone had spilt paint all over them. He had four shirts and he said they were plum, mango, banana and kiwi because he liked to call himself "a bit of a fruit."

Mr Kite made everyone laugh but Adam Burns didn't. Adam Burns was the shortest boy in Year Six but he tried to make up for it by being the hardest. Julia wasn't scared of him. She said he was pathetic.

But Jake didn't like it if he was in the boys' toilets and he heard Adam Burns come in. He just sat, hardly breathing, listening without moving until he'd gone again. Jake didn't like it any better when Adam Burns strolled into the same part of the playground. All he could do was slope off out of range, looking straight ahead and hoping he hadn't been seen.

But the worst moments were in the corridor, when Jake was walking one way and Adam Burns was heading straight towards him. The older boy kept his eyes on him as if Jake was his target and he was his own weapon ready to fire. There was no point in swerving over. Adam Burns would just swerve too. Then, just as they got so close that there was only a step between them, Adam Burns would decide. He might just laugh and say a rude word and shoulder past. But once he had barged into Jake's chest and knocked him onto one foot. He had nearly fallen over. Jake hadn't told anyone.

Not that Adam Burns took much notice of Jake most of the time. He was too busy noticing Tariq. Tariq was in Jake's class but he probably weighed a lot more than Adam. He was very heavy and his face had too much chin. Adam Burns called him "Inflatable Boy!" and once he punched him to let all the air out.

Jake thought it must be difficult being Tariq. When he ran around at playtimes he puffed a lot, like Thomas the Tank Engine going up a hill. And every swimming day he had a cold or tummy ache or virus. Tariq didn't say a word about Adam Burns but Jake knew he minded. He was just pretending not to cry inside, but crying inside was the worst kind. No one heard so no one knew. It hurt most of all.

On the first day back after half term Jake was washing his hands in the boys' toilets when Adam Burns came in. He knelt down to look under all the doors and saw the chunky ankles he was looking for. Tariq had come in at the same time as Jake and hadn't come out yet.

"I smell a porky pig," said Adam Burns. "Come on out, Porky, or I'll huff and I'll puff and I'll blow your house down!"

There was no reply but even with the tap running Jake could hear Tariq sniffling.

"If you don't come out soon I'll have to come in and make myself a bacon sandwich," called Adam Burns.

The toilet door next to Tariq's was ajar.

"Coming to get you!"

Adam went inside. Jake had no time to wonder what he was planning to do. The toilet doors rattled in a sudden draught from nowhere. Jake saw a familiar figure at his feet. The imp's mouth was set in a firm line as if *he* knew exactly what he was planning to do. One claw-like hand clutched something hidden inside it.

A moment later the imp had rolled under the door of Adam's cubicle. Jake didn't see what happened next, but he heard a squeal from Adam followed by the clunk of metal. It sounded like the bolt sliding across on the inside.

"Aaagh!" cried a weedy voice. "Get off! Let go! I want to get out!"

Tariq came out of the cubicle next-door and gave Jake a puzzled look. He shrugged his shoulders and hurried outside without daring to speak. Meanwhile Adam was not happy. But then, as he seemed to be locked in the toilet, that was not surprising.

"What are you doing?" wobbled a panicking sort of voice from inside his cubicle. "Leave that bolt alone! Help!"

The imp climbed out underneath the door, grinning. A tube of superglue was in his claw-like hand and he was laughing like air hissing out of a tyre. Jake watched as he climbed back up to the padlock on the caretaker's cupboard, turned the key and put the glue back where he had found it.

Both Jake and the imp turned to stare as the toilet door shook on its hinges. It sounded as if Adam was heaving his body at it like a fireman. Then the banging and shaking stopped and all they could hear was deep, gasping breaths. Suddenly there was a thud.

Through the gap at the bottom of the door Jake saw a hand reach out on the end of one squeezed arm. Another hand reached out before one heaving shoulder edged into the space. An ear came next, with a cheek under one eye trying to follow. Who would have thought Adam Burns could force so much of himself into that small, low gap? It was like a bird squishing itself through a hole in a fence that didn't look big enough for its head. Except that Adam wasn't made of feathers. His bones were packed with flesh and covered with sweatshirt.

There was a loud grunt. Nothing moved. Adam Burns was stuck.

The imp jumped up and down and slapped his saggy bottom. He hopped across, almost close enough to be grabbed, and grinned at Adam. He gave the eye and ear a little wave.

Jake could see the eye on the floor staring at him. It looked redder and more watery than usual. He didn't suppose anyone had ever seen either of those eyes look tearful before.

"Don't move," he told Adam, and as he hurried to get Mr Kite he tried not to laugh at his joke.

The story round the school was that the caretaker had been called in to break open the lock. Adam Burns must have had rather a long wait underneath. In afternoon assembly he sat very quietly indeed and the Head didn't have to tell him off once.

Of course Jake and Tariq were asked what had happened, but the only person who had seen for himself was Adam. Julia came home that night laughing.

"You're not going to believe this," she told Jake. "Adam Burns says he was locked in the toilet by the Lincoln Imp."

Julia snorted and rolled her eyes.

"Yeah, right," smiled Jake, and rolled his eyes too.

Jake knew the imp would be very pleased with himself. Jake was pleased too, because when he'd talked to Mr Kite about what happened, his words had been bigger than whispers in the silence. Jake mentioned the mean things Adam had said about Tariq, and Mr Kite didn't look too pleased at all to hear those.

As for Tariq, he started bringing salads and fruit for packed lunch next day. And though he did look puffed when he arrived at school, it was only because he had power-walked all the way. He told Jake he was going to use his bike a lot more in future.

Jake's mum was pleased that morning too, because Sunny slept most of the night. Over breakfast Julia said it was amazing.

"And the most amazing part is that I heard Jake singing to him, and that's enough to give anyone nightmares!"

"I didn't," said Jake.

"I heard you," said Julia. "You sounded like Mrs Grey's cat. But Sunny must be tone deaf because he was gurgling."

Jake frowned. Then he understood. The imp must have entertained his brother and sent him off into a long, happy sleep. He could just imagine him, swinging from the mobile above the crib and dancing along the wooden edges. He pictured him, one foot balancing and one doing a ballerina point. One ugly face must have been grinning at another.

"That was lovely of you, Jakey," said their mum.

Jake said he didn't sing anything so Dad said Julia must have dreamed it, but he gave Jake a wide smile.

"You can dream that dream again tonight if you like, Julia," said Mum, sipping another cup of tea.

She gave Jake his lunchbox and said there was a nice surprise in it.

"Custard?" he cried, clicking up the lid to check.

Yes! There it was, in a small tub with a spoon. Mum was smiling.

"I made it last night when you were in bed. Next time it'll be hot, with whatever pudding you want."

"Thanks, Mum!" cried Jake. It was starting to be a good day.

When Jake looked down at Sunny in the crib before he set off for school, the creased and twisty face was smooth. His tiny lips were open, but not wide enough to howl. It was as if somewhere inside his dream he was smiling too.

Chapter Six

Soon it was Bonfire Night. Because it was a Saturday, the whole family was supposed to be going to the big charity show at the cricket ground in town. They went every year and Jake's mum always made him wear a woolly hat and gloves and zip his coat up.

Sunny had a thick legless suit that was lined with red fur and about a million blankets for his pram but Mum and Dad decided it was too cold for him outside because his nose seemed rather runny. So the family that went to the cricket ground was the old family, the way it used to be, not the new one.

Ben's mum babysat for a couple of hours. Mum had her mobile in one hand all the time but she didn't call. There was no emergency. Even though the whole town was exploding with rockets, Sunny slept through the whole show. So Jake had two hands to hold whenever he wanted, just like the old days. Jake-In-The-Middle, as Dad used to call him, always ready to be swung in the air between them, landing for a whole two seconds before he was ready to swing again.

Then on the Sunday Grandad, Uncle Mike, Auntie Mo and Emily came round for a few catherine wheels, plenty of sparklers, fat sausages and baked potatoes. But Uncle Mike didn't stay long because he had to pack. Mum and Dad were talking in low voices, as if they had a secret Jake and Julia were not supposed to hear. Emily was very quiet, not bossy at all, and held on to Grandad's hand.

The clocks had gone back and it was dark enough by half past five to weave loops and starry letters in the still, sharp air. Jake loved sparklers. Emily still held on to Grandad even when she was twirling and weaving hers in the other hand. There was nothing too loud because of Sunny, but by six he was wide awake and Mum held him up to the window in case he could see the colours and the brightness. Jake saw him staring through the glass with round eyes.

"Look!" cried Emily. "He's so sweet."

Jake told Emily he always looked like that. It was because his brain was too small and nothing made sense.

When Grandad went inside Julia put her arm round Emily, and Jake could tell it almost made her cry.

"Uncle Mike has to go and work in France," Julia whispered to Jake later. "Emily's very upset. But don't say anything."

Jake wouldn't mind Sunny living in France, but he wouldn't like it if his dad had to work in another country. He tried to smile at Emily but it felt as if it came out crooked. Sunny seemed to catch the mood because he started crying so loudly that Jake was sure Mrs Grey would change her mind about babies.

Jake looked next-door to Mrs Grey's house. It seemed very dark inside, but there had been no complaints yet about noise in the garden. He wondered whether she liked sparklers, which were quieter than laughter. He thought he'd ask, in case she'd like to join in, so he slipped away. No one noticed because everyone was trying to make Sunny happy. But when he knocked there was no answer.

He heard Pet the cat screech loudly inside. He could see a light on in the hall but the rest of the house was in darkness. It was supper time but there was no smell of food. Mrs Grey never went out. Jake knocked again.

To his surprise the door blew open. The wind banged it against the wall. Claw-like hands grabbed it and shut it behind Jake. What was the imp doing now?

He was in a hurry. He scampered along the hall and led Jake into the kitchen, which was lit like Christmas by a row of tea lights on the window sill. It smelt as if the whole house had just been cleaned and polished. There was nothing out of place anywhere. It didn't feel like a home.

Down on the dark red tiles lay Mrs Grey. There was no blood, but she wasn't moving. Jake looked at the imp and the imp looked back. He grabbed the thin pale wrist and nodded the rhythm of her pulse. Jake knew that meant her heart was beating.

There was screeching and hissing from under the kitchen table. Pet was hiding. His eyes shone up at the imp as he let out a growl that was tickly in his throat. It wasn't happy like a purr. The imp and the cat stared at each other. The imp was very still. His face was cheeky but it wouldn't have frightened Samira. His eyes were like sparklers in the dim kitchen light.

Slowly the cat unclenched, stopped whining and curled up softly. Pet didn't even move when the imp waddled up close and stroked his fur with his claw-like hand. This time the noise in his throat sounded almost sleepy.

The imp jumped onto the worktop, flicked on the light and pointed. Beside one lonely mug was the phone. It smelt of polish as Jake picked it up.

He dialled nine nine nine. He told the lady it was an ambulance they wanted. He gave the address and his own name. His voice was clear and careful and he liked the way the calmness sounded. Then, as he was about to leave the door ajar and run home, the imp nodded up the stairs. There was something else he wanted Jake to see.

The imp started to climb. At first his legs stretched up from one step to the next as if he would split in half. Then a current of air raced up the stairs behind them and pushed him upwards. Jake thought it was a bit like switching on Julia's hairdryer at the back of his fat little bottom.

The imp looked behind to make sure Jake was following. The cat came too, swishing its tail softly past Jake's legs, its fur ruffled by the air.

On the landing Jake looked through a doorway. He felt excited for a moment, as if they were detectives on a case, trying to solve a mystery. He had no idea what he would find in the room. In fact it was almost empty. He saw a cot at one end, near the window. It had white lace all around it, hanging like curtains.

Jake knew there was no baby in the cot before he reached it. It was so still. Besides, the room felt so silent and old, like a museum.

The cat slunk ahead and jumped up on the white bedcover, sending the cot swinging gently and knocking the teddy on its tummy. On the wallpaper Postman Pat and Jess drove around in their red van. There was a large yellow lorry

on the window sill. Next to it was a tower of bricks, all different colours, arranged in a zigzag ready to be knocked down.

The imp made a little purr and the cat sprang off the cot again. Then he climbed up to sit the teddy back in place, swung down carefully and held the cot until it was still. He waved at Jake. But Jake wasn't feeling like a detective any more. Something felt wrong. Jake felt wrong. He shouldn't be there.

So he left the imp with Pet and ran back home.

He missed the cot out of the story (as well as the imp). It was still quite a long story, and it made him breathless when he remembered Mrs Grey on the kitchen floor. When he had finished, Grandad patted him on the back and Mum said he had been a star.

"Nice work, Jakey," said Julia.

"I would have screamed," said Emily, and Sunny did.

Jake wanted to go back to Mrs Grey's kitchen and wait for the paramedics to arrive, so his dad went with him. They played I Spy but Jake didn't say something beginning with i, even though he could see the imp under the table, stroking the cat under the chin until it purred.

"I spy," said Dad, "something beginning with h."

It wasn't the handles on the pans hanging shiny as new on the wall. It might have been ham in the fridge but Dad wouldn't let him open the door to see.

"Besides," he said, "that would be cheating. Your little spying eye is not some kind of x ray that can see through fridge doors."

"I give up," said Jake. "What starts with h?"

"You do," said Dad. "Hero!"

Jake smiled. Then he remembered Mrs Grey on the floor and she wasn't smiling. It didn't seem right to feel pleased about anything.

When the paramedics carried Mrs Grey off on a stretcher, Jake suddenly felt afraid. He hadn't been there when Grandma had her heart attack but she must have been driven away like this. But Grandma was dying and the siren must have been wailing louder than Sunny could ever manage.

"Mrs Grey will be all right," said Dad when they had gone, "thanks to you."

Jake felt tired all of a sudden. He wondered when Emily was going home, until she came downstairs in a pair of Julia's pyjamas with the legs rolled up so that she didn't trip over them. Obviously she wasn't leaving as soon as he'd hoped. But Julia didn't seem to mind her cousin sharing her room.

"I'll sleep on the floor," she said.

Mum called Julia the Sleepover Queen and reckoned she could sleep on the top of a fence. Julia didn't believe anyone who said she snored, but Jake had heard. Anyone who had ever been within a mile of Julia asleep must have heard. A dragon with a cold couldn't have been snortier. He didn't suppose Emily would get much sleep.

They talked for ages, but the conversation was rather one way. Julia did nearly all the talking. Anyone would have thought they had never met before and Julia was a chat show interviewer. Emily's answers were quiet and short. Jake tried to bury his head in his pillow and stick his fingers in his ears. Then it stopped.

But of course, that was just the start. There it was, the grunting of a large rare pig — otherwise known as the sound of Julia asleep. He only just heard it, though, because of Emily's snivelling. He was afraid she would wake Sunny if she didn't stop, so he tiptoed in and found her with the duvet pulled up to her bright, wet eyes.

"Can I come in your room?" she whispered.

"Suppose," he said, so she followed him.

He hadn't meant to give up his bed but Emily slid in anyway. So Jake sat on the red wooden chair.

"Why are you crying?" he asked.

75

"I miss Annie," said Emily.

"Is she your friend?"

Emily nodded sniffily and said that Annie lived in her wardrobe and shared her clothes. Jake didn't like to say that if the doors were shut she would run out of air in the night and die.

"There's a tunnel at the back and we go on adventures," said Emily, "to silver mountains and rainbow rivers."

"Are there monsters there?" asked Jake.

"Annie locked them in a dungeon," said Emily.

Jake thought that must spoil the fun.

"Annie's crying in the wardrobe," said Emily. "She's lonely without me."

Just at that moment there was an odd sound inside Jake's own wardrobe. It was rather like a lion yawning. Emily's eyes grew very round as the door swung slowly open.

There was the imp, wearing a pair of Jake's red pants on his head and a sock hanging from each ear. He was giggling breathily and couldn't wait to look at himself in the mirror. Looking at the small, silly reflection and the face it was pulling, Jake saw Emily behind it in the mirror. She was staring in astonishment at the imp. She could see him, and he knew it. In fact the next moment he was jumping onto the bed to shake her hand.

With one hand covering her mouth as if she was trying not to giggle or squeal, Emily watched the imp whoosh over to the curtains and climb them, like a cross between Head Case the hamster and an acrobat. Then he climbed onto the rail they hung from, and balanced from one end to the other like a tightrope walker. Every few steps he pretended he was going to fall just to hear Emily gasp with delight.

Then he turned himself upside down in Jake's wastepaper basket and kicked his legs as if he was pedalling in the air until it tipped over on its side and rubbish spilt everywhere.

"Stop showing off," said Jake.

But the imp was wearing the wastepaper basket now. It was bigger than he was, so only his fat ankles and claw-like feet were visible underneath the red plastic. He waddled around the room like a blind penguin bumping into everything.

"He's so funny!" cried Emily in a big whisper tickly with laughter.

The imp jumped free and nodded. He had a fan. He seemed to be enjoying his new audience. In fact he reached up so that she could pick him up like a mummy lifting up a toddler. Of course Emily loved that.

When the imp was up level with her face he reached forward, and for a horrible moment Jake thought he was going to bite off her nose. But he didn't. He kissed her forehead. Jake wondered whether his lips felt slobbery but if they did, Emily didn't seem to mind.

The imp had never kissed *him*. And he didn't want to be kissed either.

Emily put the imp down very gently. Then he beckoned with a claw-like finger and she followed him out of Jake's bedroom and back to Julia's. Jake padded after them.

Before she got into the bed the imp bounced on her pillow to make it comfy. Then he danced across to where Julia lay snoring on the floor. With his finger to his lips he tiptoed over the bumps in the sleeping bag until he was looking down on Julia's face. He leaned down and pulled a twisted face at her. His tongue hung out and spun around like a propeller. At once the snoring stopped.

The imp clapped himself silently and waved to Emily. With a flap and float of the curtains he was gone. Standing watching in the doorway, Jake looked across to the bed and saw Emily close her eyes. Her lips smacked softly, as if they had just tasted honey. Then they parted in a small smile.

Jake was very sleepy. Would Emily talk about the imp, or would she think she had dreamed him? It was his imp, really, but he supposed he could share sometimes. He stumbled back to bed and slept right through till morning.

When he woke up he found Emily keeping Sunny amused, pulling faces someone rude had taught her.

"I love your baby," she told him.

"Everybody does," said Jake. "You can keep him in your wardrobe if you like."

He thought she was going to say he was mean and horrible, but for a moment she looked as if she might say, "Can I really?" Then she changed her mind.

"If I had a baby brother," she said, "my daddy wouldn't go to work in France."

"I bet he would," said Jake.

He said he would make her a cup of tea if she liked, and she nodded. Then she went to the bathroom and Jake had a good look at Sunny. He was reaching up small, tight fists like a goal scorer in slow motion, and he was smiling. Dad said babies didn't really smile at people. They were just happy to be breaking wind or filling another nappy. But Jake couldn't smell anything nasty.

"I didn't mean it about the wardrobe," he told Sunny. "Or France either."

He went to make the tea.

Chapter Seven

Jake's dad took Emily home after breakfast, holding a baby doll that Julia didn't need any more. It had a very real face, wet itself and cried. But you could turn it off and it wouldn't bother anyone.

Jake had to admit that Sunny was crying less and sleeping more. Maybe the imp entertained him every night. Maybe he was just getting the idea at last.

Once Sunny was full of milk, fat-cheeked and fast asleep again, his mum phoned the hospital to ask about Mrs Grey. She hadn't died. She hadn't even had a heart attack. It turned out that she had tripped over the cat, banged her head and knocked herself out. She had hurt her leg and would need a crutch for a while.

"She'll bang on the wall with it," said Dad, "every time anyone laughs too loudly."

The hospital said she was well enough for visitors and Jake didn't think she would have any, so he asked Dad to take him that afternoon.

"Are you sure?" asked Dad, giving him a strange look, as if he'd said he wanted to change Sunny's nappy.

When they walked into the ward Mrs Grey looked very surprised to see them. She squinted from her bed and put on her glasses as if she must be seeing things.

Even when they were sitting beside her she still stared at them. Jake thought they might as well have been aliens with three dangly red eyes bouncing around on the bedcover.

"You rescued me, Jake," she said. "I need to say thank you."

She waited before saying the last two words slowly, as if they were new ones she wasn't used to. Then she stared again. Jake thought she must have used up that small vocabulary of hers. The clock in the ward ticked very loudly. He thought she might complain.

Jake's dad, who was looking hot, went to get a cup of tea. She patted Jake's hand.

"You're a good boy," she said. "Boys can't help being noisy. Don't take any notice of me and my grumps and grouches."

Jake had never looked at her so closely. She wasn't old enough or ugly enough to be a witch. Her skin was pale but quite soft, and next to the imp's wrinkles hers were just fine lines, like the ones in Grandma's flowery old china cups. When her eyes woke up he could see she wasn't so much older than Mum.

"Didn't you have any children, Mrs Grey?" Jake asked.

For a while he thought she hadn't heard. And then she sat up straight as a ruler and her neck seemed to stretch long and tight. He thought she might shout in his face: HOW DARE YOU or GET OUT OF HERE, with a pointed finger at the open doorway.

Instead she leaned to one side of the bed and pulled a photograph out of a Bible.

"William died," she said, "when he was nearly a year old."

The baby looked fat and happy. He was in the cot with white lace curtains. He must have been staring at all the Postman Pats on his wall. William Grey. Jake wondered whether there was a grave somewhere nearby where Mrs Grey laid flowers. He said he was sorry. She patted his hand again before she took the photo back. She didn't put William away until she had looked at him for a long time.

"I don't show many people," she said, "but you're special to me now. I expect you always were special. I'm sorry I didn't see it before."

"That's all right," said Jake.

He wondered. Was he special? Sunny seemed to be the special one now. But maybe everyone was special, even him.

"I'd like to look after your baby sometime," she said, "so your mum and dad can go out." She looked hard at Jake. "You'd help me, wouldn't you? I'm out of practice."

"All right," he said.

"I know lots of card games," she said.

"Cool," said Jake, wondering whether SNAP would be as much fun if you whispered it so as not to be noisy.

Jake told Dad in the car that Mrs Grey had only been angry because her baby died but he was still alive.

"Did she tell you that?" asked Dad.

"No," said Jake. "But I think she's forgiven me now."

Dad took a deep breath.

"Better forgive her too then, hadn't we?"

In the rear view mirror above the dashboard the imp danced like a bendy Elvis, wobbling with every throb of the engine. Then he nodded his head as if it was loose, like one of those bulldogs with bad teeth that Uncle Mike kept in the back of his BMW. Jake thought he was being silly, showing off again. But he carried on grinning long after the imp had vanished.

His dad turned on the radio and started singing at full volume about "loving angels instead". His head swayed like a football fan's scarf. Jake wouldn't have wanted him to sing like that in front of Ben or anyone else at school. It would be very embarrassing. But now, with just the two of them, it seemed very, very funny. Jake laughed so much his dad kept on singing, louder and louder.

Jake thought it was hard to decide who was funnier, the imp or his dad. In fact it was *imp*ossible!

Chapter Eight

The next time Jake visited Grandad he wasn't expecting anyone. Jake was supposed to be shopping with Dad but the town was too busy and the car parks were full. Christmas was coming.

"Let's go and see Grandad instead," said Dad, after a lot of sighing and driving around in slow traffic.

Jake was glad there was nowhere to park in town. Seeing Grandad was much more fun.

Jake rang the bell. Grandad didn't look as if he had brushed his hair and his chin was stubbly. His stripy pyjamas looked as if they had been kicked around the house.

"You've caught me out!" he said. "Look at the state of me. What would your grandmother say?"

Dad put the kettle on while Grandad shaved and dressed. When he came downstairs again he asked Jake to feel his chin to make sure it was perfectly smooth. Jake said it was.

"Smooth as Sunny's bottom?" asked Grandad.

Jake screwed up his face.

"Nicer," he said.

"Did I look like the beast before Beauty kissed him?"

"No," said Jake. He thought about it. "You just didn't look plugged in."

Grandad laughed and told Jake he needed someone to do that for him every morning.

"That was one of Grandma's jobs," he said.

"How did she do it?" asked Jake.

"Oh, a bit like Beauty," said Grandad. "With a kiss." He grinned. "It did go wrong one morning and I turned into a frog instead."

Even though Grandad made a *ribbit* noise Jake could tell he wasn't in the mood for jokes, not really.

In the lounge there were things all over the floor.

"Grandma's things?" asked Jake.

Grandad nodded and said he was in the middle of sorting them out. Not her clothes, because they had already gone to Oxfam — apart from the pale blue cardigan with bobbles that she had knitted last and worn most. He meant her treasures.

Dad asked whether he would like Mum to help him.

"Oh, no," said Grandad. "She's got quite enough to do."

Then Dad had a call from Mum. Julia needed taking to dancing but Mum couldn't drive her because Sunny was making it loud and clear that he was very hungry NOW. Dad would have to go.

But he left Jake with Grandad, because Grandad asked him to. So Jake offered to help with the sorting.

"Yes, please, love," said Grandad, quietly. "She'd like that."

Jake thought he looked as if all the colours inside him had faded.

"What will you do with the treasures?" Jake asked, when he saw the old biscuit tin, shiny but dented.

"Protect them from the pirates for a start," said Grandad. "Have you seen their ship sail the clouds at night when the moon is full?"

"No, really," said Jake.

But when he tried he could imagine the Jolly Roger flag blowing among the stars.

Grandad lifted the lid off with his fingernails and looked inside the tin. Jake smelt the lavender fill the room. As Grandad stirred some papers, he lifted up a dried, pale purple sprig that melted into dust as he touched it. The tin smelt like Grandma.

Grandad was unfolding letters.

"I wrote these when we were courting," he said.

Jake only knew about tennis and judges but Grandad said courting meant dating. They were boyfriend and girlfriend once.

"Long ago," said Grandad, and smiled.

There was a photo of a girl with long thin legs, and hair that looked like it had been baked. It was hard to believe it was Grandma.

"Are you sad, Grandad?" asked Jake.

"No, Jakey, I'm happy," he said, "because this girl could have chosen any of the lads to love, and she chose me."

"Of course she did!" said Jake, and put his hand on Grandad's shoulder.

There was a boot with a pink ribbon through it that Grandma had knitted for Jake's mum. It didn't look as if she had worn it and Grandad said that was because it never stayed on her foot. Her favourite game had been kicking it off so that Grandma could put it on again.

"You wait till Sunny starts that," he said.

Jake would be glad when Sunny started doing things — other things apart from crying. It would be a big improvement.

There was a photocopy of a fuzzy black screen with a white shape curled up in the middle of it. It was from the hospital. Jake had seen one like that before Sunny was born, but he hadn't been very interested.

"That's the first picture of you," said Grandad, "inside your mum, eating your foot."

Jake had a good look and grinned.

"Greedy from the start," said Grandad.

Deeper down in the tin were some older things. They were browner and their corners looked as if the air had rubbed them away. There was a faint photo from a newspaper of a small girl looking angry. Underneath it was a question: COULD YOU TAKE CARE OF MAISIE?

"Who's Maisie?" asked Jake.

"That was your Grandma's name," said Grandad.

"She doesn't look like Grandma," said Jake. "She doesn't look happy."

Grandad told Jake that Grandma's mum had not been able to look after her because she had been too young and scared. So Grandma had been put in care.

That meant growing up with lots of other children in a big house that was called a home. But it wasn't like a home at all.

"Maisie was very angry with her mother," Grandad told him. "You see, she wrote her a letter on the first day of every month and promised to visit. But she never came."

Jake frowned. Poor Maisie. He imagined her looking out of the window.

"Every day that she waited she was angry," said Grandad. "She was angry with everyone else, everyone who was not her mother, but did the things her mother should have done."

Jake felt very sorry for little Maisie who had grown into Grandma. He thought Grandad could tell because he squeezed Jake's hand. Then he was busy again, rummaging.

"Aha!" he cried, peeling a hankie from the largest object in the tin.

Jake's mouth opened. It was an imp, carved from wood and much too smooth. It was sitting cross-legged, looking naughty, but it wasn't nearly as ugly as it should have been.

"Grandma had an imp!"

"Just like this one. She found him on a desk in an office in the home, sitting on papers to stop them blowing away. She gave him a better home, a secret one under her bed."

Jake tried to picture the girl with the straight mouth and the hard eyes creeping up to the desk and hiding the carving under her jumper. He imagined her playing with it when no one was looking.

"She talked to the imp," said Grandad, "about the nasty man who hit her hands with a ruler because her fingernails weren't clean enough."

That was so horrible it made Jake angry.

"What happened?" he asked. "Did the imp get the nasty man into trouble?"

Grandad didn't tell him not to be silly. In fact, the way he looked at him made Jake feel as if he had been rather clever. Then Grandad asked him a strange question. He wanted to know whether there was a slop bucket for leftovers in the dining room when Jake had school dinners.

Jake's nose wrinkled, because there was, and it was a bit disgusting, especially when ketchup mixed with custard and sprouts.

"Well, in the home where Grandma lived they gave the children the cheapest meat, which was tough to chew and hard to swallow. And the gravy was mostly fat and water."

"Yeuk," said Jake. "Like the gruel in Oliver Twist?"

He had seen the film and knew the words to Food, Glorious Food.

"Only worse," said Grandad. "No one ever wanted more."

Jake could imagine what the slop bucket was like in Grandma's home. But Grandad said none of the children in the home understood how all the greasy slops got emptied onto the head of...

"The mean man with the ruler!" cried Jake.

Grandad nodded. Jake could just imagine the claw-like hands holding onto the bowl. He could picture the imp high up somewhere, maybe on top of a cupboard. He must have lifted the bowl with all his strength and tipped it out just as the man walked into the room.

Jake laughed because in his mind the mean man was covered in slops. Slimy gravy dripped from his hair. Lumps of meat that couldn't be swallowed slid down and got stuck on the tops of his ears.

"The man was very angry," said Grandad, "and every child in the home had to hold out both hands to be rapped extra hard with that ruler."

Jake's smile faded. It wasn't fair.

"But someone must have borrowed a camera and taken photos," said Grandad. "Someone must have sent them to the local paper. The man got the sack."

"Good!" cried Jake.

He had an idea who that someone was. He imagined claw-like hands pressing a button, and a long tongue licking an envelope.

"Was Grandma happier after that?" he asked.

"Well," said Grandad, "some people who saw the advert wanted to adopt her and give her a real home."

"Hooray!" cried Jake.

"She was all packed. But just before she left, someone found the imp in her case and said she was a thief."

"No!" said Jake. Poor Maisie. She'd only needed a friend.

"She unpacked again and stayed another year, but they took the imp away."

"I bet he came back," said Jake, "when no one was looking."

"Yes," said Grandad, "he did. Until young Maisie was chosen again, by some very kind people who wanted someone to love."

"Did they love her?" asked Jake.

Grandad said they certainly did, nearly as much as he did, but not quite, because he was the champion at that.

"The world record holder!" cried Jake, and Grandad hugged him.

Jake asked whether Maisie ever saw the imp again. Grandad shook his head. But he said she had not forgotten him.

Jake wondered whether little Maisie had blamed her mum, because really it was all her fault. So he asked Grandad.

"Sometimes she did," he said, "but one day, when she was a teenager, she had a letter from her mum, and they met for coffee. And Grandma forgave her, because she'd learned to understand."

"She loved her after all," guessed Jake.

"Yes," said Grandad. "She had loved her all the time."

Grandad said Maisie and her mum had been friends after that. They had got to know each other. Soon Grandad had met Maisie and they had got to know each other too.

"You know the rest of the story," said Grandad.

He started humming the music for Here Comes the Bride. Jake had seen their black and white wedding photos. Grandma looked very happy and her eyes were not hard any more.

"One rainy afternoon, when we had been married for years," Grandad told Jake, "we found this wooden imp in a junk shop, miles from the cathedral. Your grandma got emotional." He looked at Jake. "Do you know what emotional means?"

Jake nodded. It meant like Grandad's face as he asked the question. But he didn't say. Grandad held out the imp. Jake put his finger on the carved wooden mouth, half-expecting it to nip or giggle, or both.

"Would you like to keep it?" Grandad asked.

Jake thought Grandad might want it himself, but he said he'd already got an imp of his own. He pointed to the photo on the window sill. It showed Grandma laughing one Christmas. Her eyes were small because her cheeks were high, and her mouth looked as stretchy as the dough Jake helped her punch when she was baking bread.

Grandad and Jake made some tea together. He offered Jake a biscuit out of the tin. While the kettle was boiling Jake put the wooden imp by the front door with his trainers, so that he wouldn't forget to take it home.

As he looked through the glass onto the doorstep he saw a much chunkier and more rubbery imp jumping up and down as if the doormat was a trampoline. Jake opened the door a little. The wind bounced the imp up high, and he flipped in the air like a pancake. Jake clapped quietly so he did it again, and landed with a bow. Then he noticed the biscuit in Jake's hand. Jake held it out.

He should have known what to expect by now. The imp jumped up from the leaves as if he was on a spring. He hovered in the air even though he had no wings to flap. His teeth latched onto the biscuit. His legs dangled. For just a second he hung there, like a dog clinging to a bone, until the biscuit broke. In a blink his long tongue had wrapped around it and curled it back into his mouth. The imp landed with another bounce, as if he expected another round of applause.

As the imp rubbed his tummy it made a rumbly noise. Then the wind lifted him up and around Jake in spirals, like a staircase in a castle. When he reached Jake's head he smacked his lips together, but he didn't bite off his nose. He planted a kiss on it, and it tickled. Then Jake realised why. The imp had placed a woodlouse there.

"Very funny!" he cried, and lifted the woodlouse to safety, as far away as possible. "Run for it, you!" he whispered.

When he looked up the imp had gone.

"I didn't mean you!" he called.

From the top of the cherry tree came a sound like a toad in the bottom of a bucket. The imp did a few ape swings from branch to branch. Then he waved, but it was a different kind of wave that didn't mean hullo, or see you later. It meant goodbye.

A chute of wind scooped him up in a tiny tornado of dancing leaves. It spun a spilling trail down the drive, across the road and away. Jake was watching the stillness the imp had left behind when Grandad put a hand on his shoulder.

"All right, Jakey?"

The wooden imp was sitting quietly behaving itself on the doormat. Jake picked it up. Even though it wasn't as ugly as the real thing, he liked it a lot.

"I was thinking," he told Grandad, "that I might give the imp to Sunny when he's a bit older."

Grandad held the door ajar a moment, looking out into the garden.

"Excellent idea," he said, and winked at the wind.